The Path From The Shadows

Courtney Crawford

Outskirts Press, Inc.
Denver, Colorado

Outskirts Press, Inc.
http://www.outskirtspress.com

ISBN: 978-1-4327-3010-9

Outskirts Press and the "OP" logo are trademarks belonging to Outskirts Press, Inc.

PRINTED IN THE UNITED STATES OF AMERICA

Chapter 1
Encounter

The biggest tent seemed a prison to Azlee, though it was meant to be a small luxury. Honored though she was among these rough men, the awe and reverence they showed her only aggravated her loneliness.

She sat in front of the small mirror in her tent, combing out her long hair. Or trying to, at least. The color of an autumn pumpkin and fine as goose down, Azlee's hair also resembled a robin's nest most of the time. It tangled with the slightest kiss of a summer breeze, the smallest change of moisture in the air. As a priestess, she wasn't permitted to cut her tresses short, so she must each day battle the fine strands. In the morning, she would pull it back and tie it, but as the day went on, the locks would inevitably escape and fall forward into her face.

The young priestess studied her reflection as she combed. She did not consider herself to be pretty. Not only was her hair long and unruly, but her face seemed gaunt, nearly lost in the shadow of her too-large, solemn eyes, eyes like tea brewed for too long. Her body did not have the womanly curves it should. Her small breasts and thin hips were usually lost in the voluminous tunics that were the uniforms of her rank. At least she was permitted to wear trousers and boots; these were more pragmatic when spending long days in the saddle. Even so, Azlee's wardrobe remained limited in her eyes. As a priestess, she was forbidden to wear bright colors or pleasing patterns. The brown of the earth and the black of the night heavens were her only everyday colors, while white, the color of purity, was reserved for the most sacred rituals. Little difference it made anyway, for Azlee rarely inhabited the everyday world anymore, and where she lived, beauty carried little significance.

Finally, her task was finished. The strands of hair were tame for now. Azlee found herself too restless to sleep. She pulled her brown cloak around her shoulders and left the tent. For a moment, she stood gazing at the sky, brilliant with dazzling points of stars, the moon an enigmatic guardian shrouded in clouds. After a deep, exhilarating breath, redolent with summer blossoms, Azlee made her way down to the river. She sat on a stone on the bank, watching the swirls of the slow current, relishing this small moment of peace in her unhappy world.

She didn't recognize the man who moved past her to stand on the river's edge, just a few feet in front of her, unaware he was not alone. Azlee made no move to speak to him. She watched him from her perch with some interest. After a few moments, he turned to go back to the camp, and his gaze fell on the priestess.

"I am sorry. I didn't mean to intrude on your evening." The man's melodic voice fascinated Azlee. The unusual accent thrilled rather than irritated.

"Your presence here doesn't bother me," she replied. "I don't believe I've seen you before. You don't have the look of a soldier." She had thought *all* her traveling companions were soldiers. After all, the High Lord of Al'Klathiu had sent skilled warriors with the mission of infiltrating the Shadowed Zone to the south and destroying the wizard who ruled there. The stealth required left little room for additional travelers and supplies.

The man laughed. Azlee noticed that tiny creases appeared around his eyes and mouth when he smiled. Surprisingly, these pleased her. "I can hold my own with a sword, but I'm not one of these warriors." He moved closer and sat down beside her. His nearness startled her. She could see the clear blue of his eyes. His musky man smell filled her nostrils with intoxicating new scent. Her heart thumped so that she knew he must hear it too.

"I am Akosha Ne Laruneth," he was saying. "You may call me Akosha." Azlee forced herself to look into his face, though she thought it would be easier to run away than to endure this nervous embarrassment anymore.

"I am Azlee," she said softly.

"It pleases me to know you, Azlee."

"If you are not a fighter, what is your purpose with us?"

"I am here to improve your odds of success." He grinned at her blank gaze.

"How will you do that?"

"Your High Lord doesn't really believe that the Shadowed Wizard can be defeated with armed combat alone." But *I* am the secret weapon."

Azlee nodded, not really understanding.

Akosha Ne Laruneth was holding a small white pebble in his hand. "With this, we have a chance to defeat the wizard."

"A *rock* is your weapon?" Perhaps he had the sickness of the mind.

He smiled. Oh, that beautiful smile. "It is not merely a rock. It creates fire such as you have never seen before. White blinding fire that cannot be extinguished. The wizard won't even have time to gather his own defenses."

"How did you come by this?"

"My family has several such talismans, with a variety of uses. They are rare and precious and not without much thought are they carried away from our family home."

"And where is your family home?"

"Laruna Forest, far to the east of here. It belongs to no king. Once, long ago, it was the dwelling place of a secret brotherhood. They had mystical powers and their knowledge would put today's scholars to shame. They knew the Earth Magic, a practice which is forgotten in the rest of the world. These talismans come from their time." Akosha put the pebble into his belt pack. "This magic does not come to my family without a price. We are the guardians of Laruna Forest. We are a part of the balance there. We are aware of every blade of grass, every beetle, every interloper. The Laruneth family can never leave the forest, though when the guardians are plenty, the rest of us can travel elsewhere for a time. We know that the forest will call us back when we are needed. Often, we leave to search for wives so that future generations remain strong and healthy."

"You are not there now," Azlee pointed out. "Are you looking for a wife?" Immediately, she wished she had not said it. How brazen of her. He would think *she* was interested in becoming his wife.

He laughed again. "The wizard in the Shadowed Zone intends to take all the world's lands and bring them into the dark. There will come a time when Laruna is threatened, when the Guardians are destroyed along with all the living things. I chose to make the long journey here to give myself to the service of your kingdom. It matters not which country one calls home. We all are responsible for stopping the proliferation of evil."

Azlee nodded quietly. Despite the anxiety she felt in proximity to this man, she was enjoying herself more than she had in a very long time. No one ever talked to her like this. With comfortable companionship rather than awkward adulation.

"What is a beautiful lady like yourself doing out

here on this dangerous mission? *You* certainly don't have the look of a warrior." Her alarm must have been visible. "I am sorry. Did I offend you?"

"No, you didn't. It's just...no one has ever called me that before. Beautiful."

"Then you must have been living among blind folk."

Azlee laughed shyly, though her smile was genuine. This man from Laruna Forest was so unlike anyone she had ever known before.

"I am a priestess and Consort of Edaru. He is our god--Edaru the God of All, Edaru the Giver and Taker of Life, Edaru the Divine Sovereign. I am here to guide Sarronel's choices during our journey." Sarronel was the leader of this critical undertaking.

"How?"

"I have the gift of Sight. I see visions of events occurring in other places, in future times. Through these, I learn where danger lurks. I use this knowledge to advise Sarronel."

"I have never known anyone with that particular talent before," Akosha remarked. "It just confirms that men will never understand all the mysteries of the world. As we learn new things, old knowledge falls into the dust of ancient history."

Azlee nodded, unable to think of a suitable reply, with only half her focus on the conversation, the other half preoccupied with these new feelings stirring inside her.

"How did you choose to be a priestess?" Akosha asked.

"Choose?" Azlee couldn't keep the bitterness

from her voice. "There was no choosing. I was ripped from my mother's side at the tender age of six and forced into the Convent, with other girls in identical circumstances. From that point on, I belonged to the Priest-Mother. My purpose is now only to do her bidding." Azlee stared at her hands twisting in her lap, as the emptiness of her life threatened to overwhelm her. She would *not* cry in front of Akosha. She must not let him pity her.

"I am sorry that happened to you," Akosha said softly. He reached over and took her hand in his, caressing it gently with callused fingers. Azlee drew in breath sharply. Her scattered thoughts vanished altogether. Her cheeks burned as if she sat too near the fire on a winter night. Panicked, she could force no words from between her frozen lips.

"What is it, Azlee?" Akosha asked gently.

"It grows late." Azlee blurted. "I must go." She pulled her hand free, rushing to her feet and back toward the camp.

"Azlee, wait!" Akosha called after her. The priestess pretended not to hear him. Though she didn't look back, she knew he stared after her, for she felt his forthright gaze drilling into her back.

Chapter 2
A Stirring Heart

Azlee's days continued in much the same patterns they had since this mission began. But she knew an irreversible change had occurred. When she caught herself peering from her horse's back, trying to catch sight of Akosha, feeling the knot of disappointment in her stomach when she could not see him, she knew the change had occurred. When, for the first time in her life, she found herself preoccupied with efforts to improve her appearance, she knew the change would endure. When the loneliness of her unique rank failed to suppress the sudden lightness of her heart, she knew the change was deep in her soul, and she both welcomed and feared it.

Traveling across the southern region of the

kingdom of Al'Klathiu, it was easy to forget the chilling circumstances that had brought together a priestess and a group of warriors. Golden were the fields bathed in the sun of summer that linked the dappled thickets like a necklace along the pale, slow river. The teasing breeze carried a delicious abundance of pleasing scents that made the ordinary act of breathing a fabulous treat. Lulled by the rhythmic beat of hooves against packed dirt, Azlee found she could enjoy the journey with a respite from her loneliness.

Dusk was a light blanket over the land when Azlee dismounted, grateful for the chance to stretch her legs after long hours in the saddle. Today, the warriors and the priestess had pushed hard to put as many miles behind them as possible. In less than a week, they would reach the ancient road into the Shadowed Zone.

The priestess rubbed her horse's neck affectionately as she gulped water from her canteen. "You're tired, too, aren't you?" she murmured. The large brown eye blinked as if in agreement. Azlee smiled, taking the reins and leading her mount away from the frenzied activity at the center of the camp.

This horse belonged to Azlee personally, not the Priest-Mother. The pretty bay mare had been a gift from Lord Durst. Locating his lost little boy had been one of the first assignments she'd had using her Sight. Creatively, the young horse had been named simply Mare. In her empty, lonely world, the perky bay had become a constant, uplifting presence.

Azlee struggled to pull a heavy bucket filled

with fresh water over for the mare to drink from. She then loosened the girth and pulled the saddle off Mare's back. Turning to set it carefully on the grass behind her, she jumped back, startled, for a man she didn't recognize had approached her from behind.

"Priestess," he said. "You need not soil your hands with this task. I will care for your horse."

Making an attempt at kindness, Azlee replied, "I thank you, but I prefer to care for her myself."

"Priestess, this chore is beneath your rank. Let me take care of the horse."

"Priestess or not, I will groom my own horse," Azlee snapped. The asperity of her tone drove the soldier backward a few steps. He stood staring at her, slack-jawed.

"Go," Azlee commanded, and was rewarded with his hasty retreat. She sighed in exasperation as she set the saddle down. "You didn't want that idiot touching you, did you?" she said to her mare. She picked up her grooming brushes and set to work.

"Good evening." The familiar, melodic voice froze Azlee mid-brush stroke. Her heart began pounding in her chest again. Slowly she turned to face him.

"Akosha. I am pleased to see you." Azlee hoped she'd kept the unsteadiness from her voice.

"And I, you, Priestess." His warm smile nearly melted her body, and she leaned against Mare for support.

"Will you walk with me?" Akosha asked.

"Why?" Azlee asked nervously.

"I enjoy your company."

"Oh." Azlee smiled shyly. "When I'm finished here, I'll join you."

"Let me help you." Akosha took the comb from Azlee's hand and started working it through Mare's mane, while Azlee finished brushing the coat.

Fallen pine needles carpeted the ground in the sparse forest, muffling the sound of their footsteps. They walked close together, but did not touch.

"Is this anything like Laruna Forest?" Azlee asked.

"Laruna is much denser. The trees are so broad that eight men with hands linked could not stretch their arms around the trunks. The souls of those trees are awake and they communicate with my family when they wish. The ancient magic is in the very air we breathe. The living stone shelters us in softly gleaming caverns. The wild magic infuses them with light of ever-changing hues from our natural world. Our homes are beautiful, in a way that no other man-made dwelling can match. Laruna is like no other place in the world." His hand moved to the chain around his neck, most of which was hidden beneath his garments. He pulled upward on it. Azlee felt her wonder written on her face when the amulet was revealed to her sight, gently cradled in his palm. Her eyes couldn't even blink, so drawn were they to the mesmerizing beauty of this stone. At once it contained every color: the pale azure of the stream in early light, the softest pink of the sky just as the sun greets the world anew, the serene greens of the sun-dappled thicket. The hues sustained a shimmering ballet upon the stone, a quiet dance of fluid grace. Azlee found she had reached toward it with one hand, without intending to. She stopped that forward movement abruptly, looking up at Akosha's face. "May I touch it?" she whispered. Akosha nodded encouragement.

A stone should be cool, with unyielding surface. Any warmth it holds should be from the external source of the hot summer day. Not so with this amulet. Azlee's fingers tingled with the thrilling warmth, which she knew was from the rock itself as from a living creature. If she closed her eyes and let all thoughts out of her mind, she could almost feel the pulse of life within it.

Slowly, she opened her eyes, lifting her gaze to Akosha's face. "There are no words to describe the feelings this stirs in my soul," she said. It was true. This was reverence to rival even her love for Edaru.

Akosha's tender smile told her he felt as she did. He closed his fingers around her hand in a gentle caress. Azlee did not pull free of his hold as they continued their stroll through the trees.

"The place where you live, you called it the Convent?" Akosha asked.

"Yes."

"Will you tell me about it?"

She shrugged. "There isn't much to tell. It is a colorless, decaying fortress. Priest-Mother appropriated it seventy years ago to house Edaru's Consorts and their servants. My room is twice my own length. It contains only a cot and a small table. We eat in a common dining area. It is a cold and miserable place, though I do like the chapel and the outdoor gardens."

"So there is some pleasure in your life?" The

tone was gentle.

"Edaru is my tranquility." With that simple remark, the conversation ended. The silence between them remained serene as they drifted back to the camp.

* * *

Azlee entered Sarronel's tent, waiting for a moment until her eyes adjusted to the dim light. She delivered her information after he waved his hand, encouraging her to speak.

"Sir, my Sight shows me a troubling picture. It seems we will camp near the hidden path to the Shadowed Zone, as planned. As you know, most of the soldiers are to go south with Akosha, leaving half a dozen or so behind to guard the path and provide protection for me. But while we are waiting, a great mob of bloodthirsty denizens from the Shadowed Zone will swarm upon us and press us into battle. Never would I advise a man of your bravery and skill with sword to flee from danger, but the evil Shadowed Ones will far outnumber us, and it's possible they could destroy us all."

"This is indeed a grim vision that has visited you this time, Priestess," Sarronel said at last.

"There is more, Sir. Although it has not been revealed to me, I can deduce that if this does indeed come to pass, there will be nothing to stop this Shadowed Mob from following our remaining warriors south and destroying them. Then all hope will certainly be lost."

"If our enemies are victorious, there would be

little to stop them from razing our kingdom. However, our mission is so vital that I cannot compromise it even for the lives of my men, who look to me for wise leadership. You have said that they will engage us in battle while we are waiting for Akosha to destroy the wizard. Our hope lies with him anyway, so it will matter not if we must flee ahead of these evil creatures."

Azlee's gaze flew to meet Sarronel's eyes. "Are you suggesting that we abandon the very men who are risking their lives to save countless more?"

Sarronel shook his head. "Priestess, I fervently pray that it will not come to that. I take my responsibility for these men's lives very seriously. I'll have to think on this for a time, to search for a solution that is of benefit to us all. Go now, Priestess. I will call again for you after I have had a chance to strategize."

The sun was gliding down toward the western horizon, painting the sky with bold strokes of red and orange. A hand cupped her elbow and she knew who touched her before he even spoke. "Come with me," Akosha said. He tugged at her arm and she hurried forward with him.

He led her to a clearing away from the camp where two horses waited with bridles and no saddles. She rounded indignantly on him. "You took my horse out without even telling me!"

He nodded, unrepentant. "Come with me," he repeated. In one graceful movement, he was astride the second horse, a taller, darker horse than Mare. Azlee complied. She hadn't really been angry anyway.

"This is Chase." Akosha introduced his own steed as they meandered along. Their words were divided by long, contented silences of the kind that could only occur between two souls so very comfortable with each other.

At an overgrown hedge, Akosha turned to her with mischievous grin and dancing eyes. "Race you!" he challenged, and urged his horse into a gallop. Azlee hurried to follow suit, and soon Mare pulled alongside Chase. The priestess twined her fingers through her horse's mane and clucked her tongue at her to increase her speed. But Chase wouldn't let her take the lead. The two horses remained neck to neck all the way to the end of the hedge, where their riders finally slowed them to a brisk walk.

Azlee was laughing so hard her ribs ached as she and Akosha neared the camp again. They slid off the horses in the same small clearing where their ride together had begun. They walked off a bit, leaving the horses to graze on the damp grasses. Akosha turned to Azlee. "Are you still mad at me for taking your horse?"

Azlee laughed again. "Of course not."

"Good. I can't bear the idea of you being angry with me." Even in the dark, Azlee could see the tender regard in his blue eyes.

Looking into those eyes now, Azlee made her choice, knowing with complete certainty that what she was about to say felt right, more so than anything else she had ever done. The consequences seemed of no importance. "I am falling in love with you," she said calmly.

Azlee heard his surprised intake of breath, but had no time to think further on it, for he had stepped very close to her. With the back of his hand, he caressed her cheek. "Your beauty and strength have possessed me," he whispered to her. "I cannot now imagine my life without you at my side." Akosha then tipped his head down and kissed her mouth. Azlee swayed, gripping the strong man before her, tasting his love on her lips.

All too soon, they had to part from each other. "You must get back to your tent, sweetheart, before someone searches for you," Akosha said, holding her hand against his beating heart. After another moment standing in each other's arms, they parted for the night. Akosha returned the horses himself so that Azlee could reach her tent unnoticed.

Chapter 3
Hostility

A sun beam poured its warmth onto Azlee's face, waking her from pleasant dreams. She stretched languidly before opening her eyes. After a moment, the actuality of what she had done reached her consciousness, and her high spirits dissipated. Memories of her early life in the Convent resurfaced, reminding her of just what the Convent residents could do if she followed through on last night's reckless desires.

An angry and terrified little girl, she'd been brought to the forbidding Convent. She'd screamed and cried and kicked her little feet, refusing to participate in her schooling. She pushed food away without eating, spilled the water onto the stone floor rather than drink it. She was too young to consider that she was not the first child to attempt defiance.

It was painfully cold the early morning hour when Azlee was dragged from her cot by two strong priestesses with hard faces. They forced her into a gloomy inner chamber where the others waited. They snatched her sleeping robe from her, leaving her naked and shivering. One of Azlee's captors pushed her way through the others to tower over the frightened girl. Something vague niggled at the child's mind, for she recognized this tall woman who was both blazing beauty and icy malice. Oh yes, that was it. This perfect blonde creature had been with the Priest-Mother when they had taken Azlee from her home.

"This plain worthless girl acts with blatant disrespect for our esteemed Lord Edaru and us, His chosen wives. As the High Priestess, it is my sacred duty to compel her to see the grave error of her behavior. This rebellious streak can yet be quashed before shame is brought down on us all."

"Yes, Kishrion," the others intoned.

The priestesses formed a circle around the naked little girl, and though no hand was ever laid on her, she was made to suffer the violation of her own mind. She'd no idea know how long she endured, while her deepest inner self was laid bare and clawed and groped and humiliated. She emerged from that chamber much subdued. From then on, she was as pliable a child as the Priest-Mother could ever desire.

Priestess Azlee shook her head slowly. She knew only too well that breaking the rules of the Convent would exact a far worse punishment than that childhood misery. Oh, but she did *not* want to return to the imprisonment of priestess life. Her devotion to Edaru wouldn't be diminished if she chose another life. And she loved Akosha, and wanted to be with him. She shook her head again, still not sure what decision she would make when the time came.

Her stomach took that moment to growl loudly. She sighed, dragging herself to her feet.

The sun was bright enough to make her blink furiously several times. She nodded courteously to several of Sarronel's warriors as she passed. Immediately, one of the men --was his name Garis?-- approached her. Azlee's smile of greeting became a horrified, slack-jawed stare. He'd spit right at her feet! Before she could bring words to her petrified throat, a clod of dirt struck her temple and disintegrated. Dust covered her face and got into her mouth, making her cough. She turned in the direction it had come from, still not comprehending this behavior from men she had been traveling with in peace for so many weeks.

Suddenly Sarronel was before her. "Priestess, return to your tent!" he ordered.

"But--" she began.

"Return to your tent at once. I'll be along shortly."

Azlee nodded numbly. As she walked quickly back to her tent, she heard Sarronel rebuking his soldiers.

Anxiety would not let Azlee be still while she waited for Sarronel. She was relieved when he finally entered her tent several minutes later.

"Priestess Azlee," he began. He stopped.

"What's going on?" Azlee prodded. "Your men are hostile—"

He interrupted her. "You were seen locked in passionate embrace with our outlander ally last night, Priestess."

"That was just a kiss," she protested.

"It was *not* just a kiss, Priestess," Sarronel snapped back. "You have given yourself to the service of Edaru and thus have sacrificed the pursuit of your own desires. Everyone knows a priestess may not allow a man to lay a hand on her. How can these men trust you to be their spiritual guide when you can't even be trusted to control yourself?"

"I am still the same person," Azlee said softly. "I still have the same Sight."

"Not to them, you don't. To my men, you and your Sight are now sullied. I can't honestly say they are wrong."

"Do you wish me to return to the Convent?"

"No. We need you to stay and finish this. I've instructed the men to leave off harassing you. Also, you are forbidden to associate anymore with Akosha Ne Laruneth."

"What will you do to him?" Azlee forced the question out around a throat that had suddenly collapsed in on itself.

"Nothing. He is from a far land, and unfamiliar with our customs. He didn't know it was forbidden to touch a priestess. *You* should have been the one to tell him."

Azlee nodded, relieved Akosha would be spared punishment. He deserved none for his kindness to her.

"I advise you to remain in your tent for at least a few hours today, until my men calm down."

"I'm hungry." Azlee wished her voice didn't sound so meek.

"I will have food and beverage brought to you."

Chapter 4
Waiting

Akosha and five of Sarronel's men rode south in the gray twilight. Azlee could see Sarronel and his warriors struggling to look encouraging. Azlee watched them go, her chest tight with apprehension. She longed to rush into Akosha's arms, kiss his lips one last time, rest her head on his shoulder, and whisper her love in his ear. Because her heart was confused no more. The possibility of being forever parted from her sweetheart caused more anguish than Priest-Mother was capable of inflicting on her.

Instead of sending most of the warriors with Akosha, Sarronel kept them at his side. They were prepared to stand and fight the Shadowed militia. No matter how dire the risks. Sarronel wasn't going to leave this completely to chance, though. He had already sent a message to the High Lord, requesting additional support. The priestess had insisted that under no circumstances were they to leave before Akosha and his companions returned from the Shadowed Zone. Sarronel agreed, but she could see that he remained on edge. She knew he would rather be fighting than waiting.

Azlee spent nearly all of her time in her tent, choosing solitude over the accusing glares of the men. She could not make herself be calm. She was ever pacing, squeezing her hands together until her knuckles whitened, clenching her teeth until her jaw ached. At times, she tried to rest, falling onto her cot, physically fatigued. But her sleep was broken and not refreshing. She kicked and squirmed, entangling herself in the blankets, sweat dampening her hair and skin. She tried prayer, beseeching Edaru to bring Akosha back to her safely.

It seemed strange, sometimes, how close she had become to Edaru. Being forced into a life she had not chosen, being subjected to the cruel whims of Kishrion—these had made her hate the god whom she held responsible for her unhappiness. She had cried often, then, though not where she could be seen by the others. She had been at the Convent nearly a year when something happened to change her perception of the Divine Sovereign.

The sky was pregnant with dark clouds, scuttled about by a freezing wind. Bitter was the cold that cut through Azlee's thick cloak as though she were naked. The breath puffed from her mouth in swirls of white haze. The conditions outside were anything but pleasant, yet Azlee had chosen the icy winter rather then spend her day inside with all those who hated her and would not cease their cruel taunting.

A stone bench in the dormant garden; Azlee lowered herself gingerly onto it, braced for the icicles of pain that snaked the length of her body upon contact with its surface. While her teeth chattered, she hugged herself tightly in an effort to slow her shivering. Did she still have a nose and two ears? The answer was unclear to her, for she had ceased to feel them on her windswept face.

The sleeping garden was a palette of all the colors of winter—dead grays, uninviting icy blues, dull washed-out beiges, glinting whites. The dismal courtyard echoed the dismal heart of the young priestess.

A flurry of movement on the peripheral of her vision drew the girl's focus outward. A rather large wolf had padded into sight with an absence of footsteps. Fascinated rather than frightened, Azlee watched as the animal approached and settled on its haunches right in front of her. Each regarded the other. The priestess took in the way the gray and white of his coat mingled to form a lustrous silver, the black moist nose, the tongue that was a pink ribbon reaching lazily for the ground.

She wanted to touch him. (She didn't know why, but she just *knew* this was a male, a proud king among beasts). Timidly, she reached forth as if to do so, then stopped, not sure if she could complete the motion. The beast neither backed away nor nuzzled up to her hand to claim the caress. She let her fingers touch the crown of his head, gliding them gently over the gleaming silver briefly before withdrawing her hand. How *could* a simple animal's pelt feel so delicious, so divine?

The brown eyes contained intelligence; no unfair judgments lurked within. How remarkable that a wolf could look upon her this way while her own kind could only perceive her through the veil of their own resentment. Azlee noticed an unfamiliar sensation, and realized it was the corners of her mouthing tugging upward. The wolf remained unperturbed while the young priestess shot to her feet and raced to get back inside. She didn't even realize that she pushed Kishrion roughly aside in her haste to get to the private chapel where the girls were permitted time alone with Edaru. Falling on her knees before the altar, she listened to the beating of her own heart for a few long, glorious moments. The huge grin had not come off her face since she'd left the garden. Soon she collected herself and began talking to Edaru from her heart for the first time since her arrival at the Convent. It had taken a simple wild beast for her to realize that Edaru was not her enemy. He was her friend, her family, her betrothed. Did he also sometimes wear the shape of a wolf in winter?

* * *

Gray clouds scuttled across the night sky. The stiff wind chilled Azlee so that she shivered suddenly. She pulled her cloak tightly around her slim body, quickening her step. She was headed for the fire and the cooking pot. She'd had a hard time getting food down these last days. Her anxiety kept her

25

stomach roiling with spasms, driving her appetite away. Tonight she was determined to eat something, hoping it would help her rest a bit.

"Good evening, Priestess." The cook for the night, Arzogan, welcomed her as she approached. His kindness was genuine; most of the men had dispensed with anger and resentment as the days passed, treating her with renewed warmth and respect.

Arzogan held out a bowl of stew to the priestess. "Thank you," she said, reaching to take it from him. Involuntarily, her forearm struck the side of the bowl with enough force to send it arcing through the air before it hit the ground with a hollow thud. Blinded by the unnatural white flame that filled her vision, she could only stand, not daring to attempt movement. Staring right into the sun magnified a thousand times might come close to this experience. Fire consumed her eyes, forging a path of unbearable pain. She closed her eyes but the unnatural blaze remained unaffected. Her hands flew to her eyes. She cried out in her confusion. She barely noticed when she fell in a lurch to the cold ground.

"Priestess, Priestess!" The voices floated around her head. She felt arms around her shoulders, heaving her into a sitting position. Someone was babbling like a terrified child. Belatedly, she realized that it was she who was spewing forth that river of words. She fought to exert control over herself, though the struggle was excruciating. Groping with one hand, she grasped the first person that came to her touch.

"Sarronel!" she cried. "Take me to Sarronel!"

"To Sarronel! Bring the Priestess to Sarronel's tent!" Strong arms pulled her to her feet. She clung to those nearest her, stumbling along as they led her to the leader's tent.

Azlee heard Sarronel's voice as though from a great distance. "What is this?" he demanded.

"Sarronel, please!" Azlee cried. "I must tell you of the vision that now grips me!"

"Let her lie down!" Sarronel shouted. Azlee was gently lowered onto cushions on the floor. She lay silent for a moment, her chest heaving, her breath coming in short gasps. Gradually, she was able to relax, and as she did, she realized that the pain was receding. A slow smile curved her lips. The meaning of the vision was now clear to her.

"I have seen the white fire," she whispered. "They have destroyed the wizard!" The relieved cheers of those within hearing reached her ears, and her smile widened.

"What should we do now, my lady?" Sarronel inquired.

"We wait for our saviors to return, and remain ever watchful for our enemies on the approach."

"Then wait we shall!"

The whole camp agreed whole-heartedly they should wait for their liberators to return. The air in the camp was alive with the flower of renewed hope. For a while, everyone in the camp shared the same unwavering faith in imminent victory.

Within a day, Azlee regained her vision. Lingering outside the perimeter of the camp, she paced restlessly for hours at a time, searching for riders returning from the south. Her heart sang; though she missed Akosha terribly, she knew that she would soon be back in his arms.

* * *

"How long before they reach us?" Sarronel asked.

"I don't know," Azlee replied. She sounded calmer than she felt.

"How many?"

"There are at least five of them for every one of us. They are a force sent from the Shadowed Zone before the wizard died. Their purpose is merely to destroy, bringing the shadows to our bright land. They are not aware of us yet, but I am certain that this camp lies in their direct path."

"Then we have no choice," Sarronel said, sighing. "We must leave from here immediately. We can no longer wait for reinforcements."

"Do you intend to leave Akosha's group to be slaughtered upon their return?"

"We no longer have the luxury of waiting for them, Priestess. I have the lives of *all* my soldiers to consider."

"They have saved us!" Azlee protested. "How can you abandon them now?"

"What would you have me do?" Sarronel snarled. "We don't even know if they are still alive! If we stay here it would just be more wasted lives."

Azlee could think of nothing to say. Sarronel's responsibility for the warriors and the priestess entrusted to his care would make either option bitter to his taste. Sarronel wanted only to do what was right.

Oh, but she missed Akosha so. How could she leave here without knowing he was safe?

"My lady," Sarronel said gently. "Please believe I don't want to leave Akosha and my soldiers who are with him. They have risked all for the benefit of so many. Yet I see no other way."

"Lord, I offer you a compromise," Azlee said finally. "We wait until dawn tomorrow to break camp. If the men are back by then they will ride with us. If they are not, we ride for reinforcements and return for the soldiers as soon as we are able."

"What if the mob arrives here before dawn?"

"Then we must all pray to Edaru for our lives."

"Very well," Sarronel agreed. "We leave at dawn."

Chapter 5
Into the Shadows

Mare snorted, her breath a puff of white in the dawn chill. The creaking of leather and the jingling of harness reached Azlee's ears as Mare kept pace with the leading horses. The grief that consumed Azlee's heart had to be ruthlessly squelched so she would not shout at Sarronel to stay. She'd made the compromise with the leader and must uphold her part. She stared at the ground as it passed swiftly beneath the mare's hooves. She would not weep now.

Hearing a cry from the rear of the line, she twisted backward. The soldier directly behind her met her eyes, unalarmed. Azlee shrugged, dismissing the sound as innocuous, when more cries cut the crisp morning air.

"Stop! Stop the horses! Sarronel, come quick!"

Sarronel broke from the front of the line, racing past on his big black mount. Azlee turned Mare so she wouldn't have to crane her neck to see what was happening. For a moment she saw nothing out of the ordinary. Then her eyes grew wide and her hand flew to cover her mouth.

From the south, three humans struggled toward them. They were on foot, one man's arm across another's shoulder. Even from this distance, Azlee recognized her beloved Akosha.

"Akosha!" she cried, forgetting for the moment the restriction placed on her. She touched Mare's sides with her heels, desperate to reach her dear one's side. The soldiers before and behind her aborted the attempt.

"No, Priestess," she was told. "They will be looked after." Azlee had no choice but to obey.

A few minutes later, Sarronel reappeared to take his place at the head of the line. The horses started forward again. Azlee wanted to scream at them. *What are you doing? How can you leave them?* Knowing it would only make them angry, she held her peace. She must think of another way to help Akosha.

"…will treat Akosha and his companions with the honor they deserve." Sarronel's words drifted into Azlee's inward-turned mind, seizing her attention. Sarronel continued. He didn't notice the priestess, straining her ears to catch his words. "I've left some of you with them to escort them at a slower pace. They are much weakened."

Azlee exhaled softly. Akosha would be safe, after all.

* * *

Her eyes snapped open. She rose in silence and drew on her cloak. Standing in the middle of her tent, she tried to order herself back to bed. But something was calling her, and wouldn't be denied.

She managed to avoid being seen by those on watch as she hurried toward the thick cluster of trees on the water's edge, uncertain why that was her destination. A dark figure stood a few yards from her.

"I had hoped you would find your way here tonight," the melodic voice said. He held his arms out and Azlee rushed into them, wrapping herself around the strength of his body. He stroked her hair, lips touching her head. For long moments, Azlee couldn't tear herself from Akosha's arms. All too soon, though, he pushed her gently away without letting go of her, and looked into her eyes.

"I have to go back, Azlee," he said softly.

"Go back?" she echoed, staring at him without comprehension.

"The wizard's talisman is still there somewhere. I must retrieve it, or someone else will find it for himself. You aren't safe until the talisman is destroyed."

Azlee shook her head in mute terror, backing away from her sweetheart, as if by putting distance between them she could negate the truth of his words. He came close to her again, placing his palms against her cheeks in sweet caress. She closed her eyes. She couldn't think of him walking into danger again, after having barely survived the first time.

"Stay with Sarronel," Akosha bid her. "His warriors will protect you from harm."

"I will wait here for you!" Azlee cried.

"No, it isn't safe. Go with them. I will find you."

Azlee nodded, choking back sobs. Akosha tipped her chin up and landed a rough kiss on her mouth. She leaned into him, returning his kiss so ardently her lips were bruised. Then he was gone, and she crept back to her tent to weep into her pillow.

* * *

The town of Silver Mist nestled in a valley and crept up the surrounding slopes. Sarronel left his men to their own pursuits for a time. He had already sent another rider to intercept his reinforcements. He wanted them all to gather at this small town to work out the details of their attack. He was determined to search out that mob of evil creatures and vanquish them decisively.

When Sarronel told Azlee that she would not need to report to him over the next several days, the first thing she decided to do was take a bath. She had a room all to herself at the Inn of Dreams, and she found she could float on the scrumptious cloud that was her bed. A round-faced, rosy-cheeked matron named Dantra had appointed herself Azlee's handmaid. The older woman wasted no time in drawing a steaming bath and scenting it with clover and mint leaves. When she was quite alone, the priestess disrobed and lowered herself into the water with an ecstatic sigh.

She didn't get out of the bath until her body withered and the water cooled to tepid. She'd scoured every inch of her body, including her hair and scalp, to strip away the grime from long days of travel. Dressed in a clean gown, she settled in to work the tangles out of her uncooperative hair.

Once she was clean, and her belly full of roast mutton and root vegetables from the kitchen, anxiety over Akosha's fate pushed its way to the forefront of her mind again. Restless, she wandered outside, making her way past the neat rows of houses and shops. With her hand, she shaded her eyes from the lowering sun, peering up at the hillside, the bulk of which limited her view. After a moment, she shrugged and began climbing the grassy slope.

At the top, Azlee paused for a few moments to let her breathing and heartbeat slow down. The climb had been more challenging than she'd thought it would be. She settled herself on the grass, facing south, and hugged her knees to her chest. She couldn't discern the location of the overgrown route into the Shadowed Zone, even from this height. No dark-haired rider with crystal-blue eyes could be seen approaching.

"My beloved, my beautiful..." The melodic voice floated into her awareness. For the briefest moment, her spirit soared, but quickly its wings were broken. Azlee sagged into dejection, for she knew it was only the longing of her heart that had given voice to the wind. She rested her cheek

against her thigh and released all the sobs that she'd suppressed. She made no attempt at discretion; it mattered nothing to her who witnessed this loss of control. Her body shook with the force of her grief, the tears soaked her face in saltwater. And still she wept. When the stars made tiny pricks of light against the night's velvet backdrop, Azlee continued to cry desolately. It was only when the night chill crept into her bones and she found her shaking had more to do with temperature than grief that she tried to clean her face with her scarf. It took some effort to get to her feet as her body had stiffened while she'd sat. She hurried to get back to her cozy room.

* * *

Banging on the door roused Azlee from the blissful unawareness of sleep. All the pain and loneliness returned to drag down the corners of her mouth.

The knocking grew more insistent. "Priestess," someone called. "You have a visitor here. He just arrived this morning."

Immediately, Azlee's heart began thudding within her ribcage. She caught her breath, but couldn't stop the smile that burst onto her face.

"I'll be down as soon as I'm dressed," she called, already rushing around the room to make herself lovely for her beloved's return.

When Azlee opened her door a few minutes later, she found a demure child of no more than fifteen years, her thick black hair plaited down her back. Azlee recognized some of this girl's features, and concluded she was the daughter of the inn-keeper, whom the priestess had met upon her arrival here.

The quiet child led her down the stairs and pointed into the main dining area. "He is waiting for you in there. I must start my day's work now, so Papa doesn't get angry." The girl bowed quickly to the priestess before hurrying away. Azlee spared a small smile for the becoming child.

The common room was nearly empty this late in the morning. She saw four of Sarronel's men deep in conversation at a table. They waved in acknowl-edgement, but did not invite her over. Then she saw the man sitting quietly in the corner, a steaming mug on the table before him. Bitter disappointment cut her like a weapon when she recognized the markings of the Convent. For a long moment, she could not move forward. Her heart beat raggedly; she felt weak with the impact of her disappoint-ment. Finally, she squared her shoulders and ap-proached him.

"Brother Pairey, what are you doing here?" Brother Pairey had served Priest-Mother with un-wavering loyalty since before Azlee had arrived at the Convent.

"I have come to escort you back to the Con-vent," he replied.

"What of Sarronel?" Azlee asked.

"Sarronel is about to lead his men into a bloody battle and would not endanger you by bringing you along. There would not be time to hear your advice at any rate."

Azlee nodded. "I'll get my things," she said

hoarsely, and fled upstairs.

Heading due east toward the Convent, Azlee put forth much effort to keep from sinking into despair. She reminded herself repeatedly that Akosha had promised he would find her. What more obvious place could there be for him to seek her out than the Convent, after all? Nonetheless, leaving the warriors she had served in their common purpose left her feeling as if she was leaving behind the last vestiges of her time with Akosha.

The dusk shadows had deepened and the weight of her eyelids grew considerably. Hunger gnawed at her belly, too.

"I'm exhausted, Pairey. Please, let's stop for the night."

"Priestess, we must push on. There will be a warm inn with a hot meal up ahead."

"The weather is temperate enough, and I can eat bread and cheese. I am well accustomed to camping outside." Azlee was not entirely successful in keeping the irritation from her voice.

"As you wish, Priestess," Pairey replied.

Before long, the pleasant smell of burning wood filled Azlee's nose as she laid out the blankets on the flattest piece of ground. The campfire crackled, licking the deep blue night with flame the color of Azlee's hair. Staring into the fire, Azlee's thoughts again turned to her beloved Akosha. Where was he? Was he alive? Was he safe? There were no answers to these questions, and Azlee's heart grew heavier. There would never be another man like her Akosha.

"He thought I was beautiful," she said to herself.

The barest whisper of sound reached her ears.

She turned to find Pairey staring at her with fur-rowed brow, the freshly filled water canteens forgotten in his arms. "I'm sure there are many who see you as beautiful," he said, surprised. "But a priestess is a woman of such purity and piety that she has given herself to Edaru himself; a man would be eternally shamed to tell her that her physical form excites him." Pairey finally remembered the canteens he was holding and set them down nearby. "Make no mistake, Azlee," he continued. "You *are* beautiful."

Astounded, Azlee could only stammer out a shy thank you. These words were so unexpected from the usually reserved Pairey. The fine compliment buoyed her spirit.

* * *

In the darkness of a moonless night, Azlee hurried to clasp a black cloak around her shoulders and stuff some rations into her carry sack. She was careful not to break the silence; she didn't want to alert her sleeping escort. Her heart was frozen in terror but her mind and body were purposeful. For she had Seen Akosha, damaged nearly beyond recognition. He had reached out to her with one shaking hand, pleading for her help with a mouth that made no sound. Azlee could not for a moment consider abandoning him.

Mare whickered softly at her, submitting to the weight of the saddle and the restraint of the bridle. With swift grace, Azlee swung onto her horse's back. When the distance had widened between the rider and her sleeping companion, the priestess urged Mare into a gallop.

Azlee knew it would take many days to back-track to where Akosha had twice crossed the border south. What she didn't know was exactly *when* what she had seen in her vision would come to pass. So she urged her mount to cover as much ground as possible by day, and rested for only four hours at night. She would *not* cause her horse to founder, and she would *not* trade her dear equine friend for a fresh steed.

Mare hung her head; her ponderous footsteps pulled her equally exhausted rider along the dusty road through the village of Atro. Azlee stroked her sweat-soaked neck, trying to convey encouragement.

"It's not much farther now," Azlee told her. "And you'll get a warm stall and a nice helping of alfalfa." She peered ahead, looking for the chapel of Edaru. "Oh, there it is."

Two women emerged from the interior of the chapel as Azlee dismounted.

"Honored Lady!" the first one exclaimed, arriving at Azlee's side. Her round face beamed cheer-fully up at the priestess. Despite her fatigue, Azlee couldn't help giggling at the older woman's comical face. She just looked so *happy* to see a bedraggled priestess dragged up in her courtyard.

The other woman gestured to a lanky, tanned girl child with two braids plummeting down her back. "Take the horse please, Lita." While the girl obeyed, leading Mare to the small barn out back, the second woman fell in with them as they moved toward the house. "It's just we get so few of you ladies out this way," she explained. "Temretha always enjoys visitors from the Convent. I'm Ralia, by the way."

Edaru in gleaming bronze presided over the dim room. Closing her eyes, Azlee inhaled the sweet cinnamon swirls of incense that hazed the air. Opening them a moment later, she noted with approval the dried gardenias that had been strewn along the walls to promote peace and harmony in the chapel.

"You'll be wanting a hot dinner, I expect," Temretha said. "Come, the kitchen's back here."

A roast hen with fresh summer squash and corn seemed the most delicious meal of Azlee's life. It was hard for her to curb her appetite enough to keep her manners. She really didn't have to stuff everything down her throat as if it was her last meal.

They showed her a place she could rest for the night. It was quite a small room, but there was a cot with clean linen, so it was more than satisfactory to the road-weary priestess.

"We can't offer you a proper bath, Honored Lady, but we can give you a bowl of hot water and a clean cloth if you want to wash up that way," Ralia said.

"I would like that, please."

Ralia nodded, bustling out of the room.

After her "bath", she put on less soiled clothing and went back to the chapel proper. She didn't see her hostesses. She knelt on the cool stone floor before the likeness of her Husband, pausing to clear her mind and get her thoughts in order.

"Edaru," she finally murmured. "Long have I been your faithful Consort. I love You above all else in this world. I am Your loyal servant in the physical world. Now I must pray to You for guidance for there is something that troubles me. A man has stirred my heart to passionate love. It violates my vows to You, my Divine Sovereign, yet I no longer seem to have control over my desires. I ask, what would You have me do?"

She closed her eyes then. She kept her mind clear to be ready to receive Edaru's response should it be forthcoming. She ignored the protest of her back and knees, the cold that crept into her legs.

Almost an hour passed before she stirred again, opening her eyes. "Oh Wise Edaru, I beseech you to keep Akosha safe. I will do as you wish."

It was morning again, and Temretha and Ralia wore twin expressions of caring concern. Azlee hugged them both. "I will never forget your kindness," she promised. Beside her, Mare snorted. Her comfortable night had gifted her with renewed vigor.

Temretha pressed a carry sack into her arms. "Honored Lady, we don't know what you are heading into, but you may find you can make use of these."

Ralia continued. "In that bag you'll find sacred herbs and a vial of Blessed Water. There are even some additional cloaks of your office that were left here long ago. They are clean, anyway."

"And some provisions for the road," Temretha offered.

"Thank you. Edaru will shine His Light upon

you both."

With reluctance, Azlee put herself in the saddle again. She hated to leave this haven of peace and companionship, but Akosha needed her.

Late afternoon on the fifth day brought her to the end of her journey in the peaceful kingdom of Al'Klathiu. Azlee looked around at this place where she had had to say goodbye to Akosha not once but twice. It seemed so desolate now. She shivered and hugged her arms against her chest.

Down by the river bank, where she had first laid eyes on the man she would come to love, she scooped up the tar-like mud in her palms and packed a good amount of it onto her face and neck, spreading more onto her hands and wrists. Then, sighing, she got up onto Mare's back yet again, pulling the hood of her black cloak as far around her face as possible. Finally, there was nothing left to do but head into the Shadows.

Chapter 6

Rescue

Azlee peered down at the wide, well-worn road from her dubious hiding place behind some spiny, malodorous shrubs. She listened with her heart in her throat as the synchronized footsteps grew louder. Marching, they came. How many? Maybe fifty or so. They had the general shape of humans, but the dull black armor made it impossible to tell for sure. Even the bulky helmets obscured every-thing tell-tale about them. They advanced in perfect rows, a moving crop of shadows. They were headed north. North to Al'Klathiu.

Azlee remained frozen long after the troop had passed by and the road lay empty once more. She scanned her location, noting the creepy, misshapen trees—bare of foliage—that passed for a forest here.

If she were careful to avoid the dangerous clumps of needle-bearing bushes, she could travel through the woods and remain unseen. Drumming up some courage, she guided Mare forward through the trees paralleling the open road.

As they sped along their frightful route, perhaps Edaru did protect them, for Azlee and the mare arrived without notice at the charred ruins of the wizard's palace. A darkness most foul engulfed Azlee, and she clenched her teeth tightly so as not to give in to her sudden compulsion to vomit. The need to reserve her strength overrode her queasiness. She fought to stay on guard against the near-tangible evil that threatened always to derail her.

Even through the murky atmosphere, it didn't take long for Azlee to realize this wasn't Akosha's location. But this was where he'd expected to find the wizard's talisman. Where, then, had he gone?

With much effort, the priestess suppressed the panic blooming hideously within her heart. Closing her eyes, she chased all thought and emotion from her mind. She began praying fervently to Edaru, the God of All who had been her divine guide and protector always without fail.

Water. So much water, deep and cold, dark and sinister. It was not the gentle, laughing water of the streams from home. Evil had changed its very chemistry, so that now it was nearly alive with its compulsion to destroy. This water with malicious intent lapped up against a wooden platform, greedy for the thing which lay there, maddeningly out of reach of the dark water's power. But it would wait, bide its time, for there must come a moment when that motionless thing did approach too close to the water's edge...

Azlee's eyes opened slowly, and she found her palm against her mouth. She shuddered violently, remembering the horror of the dark water's intent. Remembering that it had lusted after an innocent, a young man...A gasp escaped her lips, for she realized the human on the platform had been her Akosha. She would find him at the docks then.

Akosha had suffered a terrible beating, a secret which his swollen, blackened face gave away at once. His wrists and ankles were bound too tightly; fierce red welts betrayed this. His eyes were closed; they didn't open when Azlee called his name with soft desperation and shook him vigorously. When she finally admitted to herself that her beloved wouldn't wake right now, she turned away in frustration. She stepped forward to collect Mare from her hiding place along the sagging warehouses. A hand clutched her sleeve, aborting her forward motion. She whirled. But he still slept. She frowned, puzzled.

"Talisman..." he suddenly moaned. "Find the talisman."

Though he couldn't fight his way back to consciousness, Akosha had, in his deepest inner self, recognized that a creature of Light had come near him. For the briefest moment, he had succeeded in tearing himself from underneath evil's oppressive thumb to cry for help.

Azlee looked around, slowly turning her body in a circle. How should she begin to seek the talisman of dark power?

Darkness emanated from a small cargo ship in such waves that Azlee could barely draw breath into her lungs. This, then, was where the talisman hid. She reluctantly left Akosha, and crept up the rotting gangplank. Trepidation stopped her breath as she entered the shadows inside the ship.

Each step the priestess took forward was a tremendous effort, as the cloud of menace that coalesced around her bent its will to the task of driving her back. Azlee closed her eyes, clenched her teeth, fixed Edaru's image firmly in her mind, and pressed on.

In the captain's cabin, a dull, black mass felt solid, but to the naked eye it seemed to writhe and twist in a vile similarity to a living, slimy quagmire. Azlee's stomach roiled with violence. Quickly, she wrapped the wicked charm in a kerchief and slipped it in her pocket.

Men's voices put her on sudden alert. She crept to the tiny slit in the wall and peered out. Akosha still slept where she had left him. Two scruffy-looking men, both with black beards and brawny bodies, had appeared on the dock. Each of them picked up a crate from the piles of cargo strewn haphazardly beyond the edge of the platform. They headed directly for the boat. As her thoughts raced to find a solution to her frightening dilemma, the conversation between the two thugs reached her ears.

"There's a lot of cargo here, Dezze," the slightly shorter one said nervously.

"So? We've had a lot more than this before. Never had any problems getting the job done."

"It's not the job what's bothering me."

"Well, what then?" Dezze demanded.

They were near the top of the gangplank now, and Azlee could no longer pay any attention to their words. Quickly, she crept over to the side of the boat nearest the wide bay. Climbed over the railing. Slithered down the ladder that clung to the side of the vessel, stopping about halfway down to cling like a barnacle and wait for the way to be clear again.

"Don't you feel the shadows moving, Dezze?" the shorter one asked in a low voice.

"I don't feel anything but what I always feel, you imbecile. There're always shadows here. You know that."

"It's not the same this time. Stop a minute. You'll understand what I'm trying to tell you."

A pause and then a thud when they set the crate down.

"What is that?" Dezze finally whispered. "It's like...an evil bigger than what we already know is chasing me, and I can't get away. It's wrapping around me and won't let go. It'll consume me..." His voice of madness faded out, but the fear did not.

"C'mon, Dezze. Let's get out of here."

The priestess waited for an endless time after the noises of these men receded. She began climbing back up the ladder. She sighed, relieved, when her hand reached the top, and she heaved herself upward one last time.

Panic flooded her—her left foot had slipped off the rung. She grabbed wildly at the sturdy railing, but with no success. As she plunged into the dark waters, she bit her lip to keep from screaming. Then icy water washed over her head.

The water was a force of malice all its own; this she had Seen. Now it turned its own dark hate against her, turning the consistency of thick paste that she couldn't swim through. Though her first instinct was to flail and flounder until she was sapped of all strength, she forced herself to remain still. That was the quickest way to defeat.

She began to chant a litany within her mind, a rhythmic spell to wield as a weapon.

I am a woman of Light. Darkness cannot claim me. She refused to panic, though now the urgent demand of her body for more air made her long to open her lungs, no matter that she would drown rather than breathe. She controlled this instinct, clinging to her words of courage. *I am a woman of Light. Darkness cannot claim me.*

Forever and more passed in Azlee's mind before the water that imprisoned her gave way. It was only a marginal gain, but the priestess pressed her advantage and, without breaking her chant, she forced herself to the surface of the bay. Immediately, air burst into her lungs, and, tainted though it was with the evil of this place, it was still like mother's milk after so long submerged.

As soon as she had pulled herself from the water, Azlee rushed to lead Mare as close to Akosha as possible. He still didn't respond when she attempted to rouse him. With grim determination, she hooked her elbows under his arms, dug in her heels, and pulled as hard as she could. Akosha budged only two or three inches. The priestess repeated her attempt, and again, he barely moved. She looked up at her saddle. How would she ever get him on her horse?

"Who is that?" The demanding voice caused Azlee to twist around so quickly that she landed on her hind end with a surprised grunt. Scrambling to her feet, she faced the man across from her.

"What are you doing here, Brother Pairey?" she demanded in turn.

"I tracked you here, of course. You're under my care and I'm not going to let you just slip away by yourself. Now, tell me, who is this man?"

"This man is the hero who destroyed the Shadowed Wizard," Azlee explained, impatiently.

"You risked your life for a fool!" Pairey spat.

"He is not a fool!"

"Oh? While I was waiting for you in Silver Mist, your comrades told me the story of their success. They said he was responsible for their lives, thanks be to Edaru. Yet he willingly journeyed back into this realm of darkness, and you are the fool who followed him!"

"He was coming for this!" Azlee jerked the kerchief out of her pocket and unfolded it, thrusting the talisman under Pairey's nose.

Pairey turned pale; he hastened backwards a few steps. He held his hand up as a defensive shield. "Put it away," he whispered. "Please. Just put it away."

The priestess complied, speaking to Pairey in a calm voice. "This is a talisman of power, Pairey. Akosha came here to retrieve it so it could be destroyed. If left here, it will all too easily fall into the hands of one who is the enemy of the Light, and it would finish us. Akosha is a man of courage. He is no fool."

Pairey nodded abruptly. "Let's get moving, then. The hero will ride with me." Together, they lifted Akosha's heavy body onto Pairey's larger mount.

Expediency became their only ally. The talisman in Azlee's pocket became a magnet of abomination, drawing evil swiftly after them. Her Sight showed to her the way ahead closing itself to their passage, so as not to let precious prey fly to freedom. The very nature of the horses' movement changed; for every time a hoof struck the ground, and the powerful legs lunged forward, a great invisible hand pushed them back, so that the riders on their horses made little progress.

Now was not the time to wait passively for the Sight to light her path. The priestess, chosen of Edaru, must call on every scrap of power that she could bring to her hand, she must lay herself open and vulnerable in order to reach reservoirs hidden deep within her. One quick glance was all she spared for those who were her companions on this frightful journey. After that, she had to force them out of her awareness, sinking into the realm of the spirits where her work must now be done. She brought the brightly burning image of Edaru with her to combat the shadowed phantoms, hungry to feast on the blood of creatures of Light.

At first it was as if two large, strong hands gripped her head and face, pressing hard one against the other. She felt her head had been trapped in a tremendous vice; the pressure steadily increased. The space allowed for her own brain continued to give way. Dull red like old blood crept into Azlee's field of vision, accompanying the excruciating torment. There could not exist more pain than this. No, this thought had formed too soon. For the invisible vice now grew in size so that Azlee felt the awful squeezing the length of her whole body. She felt sure her ribs would splinter; already, she was suffocating.

She was so tired, and all she wanted was to sleep, sliding into gentle darkness. How easy that would be, how relaxing, how liberating.

Her hold on consciousness had faded nearly altogether, but something niggled at her memory. It was irritating. She couldn't sleep until she figured out what it was. Oh, but she was so tired. Why couldn't it wait until later, when she was rested?

For a fleeting moment, clear blue eyes appeared in her mind and then vanished. Her heart hardened with fury and she bared her teeth as a wild animal does when defending her young. She summoned forth every last reserve of energy and power she could from her slight body and her formidable mind.

A blazing white aura crackled to life from within her. She struggled to infiltrate her formless enemy, and experienced the backlash as the shadows thrust themselves back at her with full force. For endless moments it was as if all time had stopped. Her movements, arrested. Though pain continued to consume her body, Azlee did not again falter. The power of Light that she herself had the use of shone forth.

Freedom returned to Azlee's limbs, bringing a smile to her face. The shadows were fleeing. On the heels of that optimistic observation, Azlee returned to herself in the physical world. The horses suddenly regained the ability to stretch their legs in an all-out gallop. Not two strides forward, Azlee collapsed against Mare's neck.

Chapter 7
Battle the Talisman

Something was tickling her nose. It smelled pleasantly of summer. Cautiously, she opened her eyes, groaning as the sunlight reached them, tender as they were after so long in near darkness. The priestess rolled slowly onto her side.

Her itchy mattress turned out to be a wide stretch of grass, mottled brown and green by the summer sun. Several large footsteps away, she found Akosha too lying on the earth, unmoved by the hot sun or the chirps and buzzes of birds and insects nearby. She was grateful that someone had taken the time to try to make him comfortable, placing a cloak beneath his head as a makeshift pillow, another one loosely across his body.

Azlee sat up quickly, and immediately wished

she had not. Nausea and dizziness claimed her body; she had to be quite still and breathe deeply and slowly for several long moments to keep her stomach from heaving.

"Here, drink this." Pairey thrust a water canteen under her nose.

"Where are we?" Azlee croaked, after gingerly taking some sips from the canteen.

"About seven or eight miles out of the Shadowed Zone. You two simply could go no further, and the horses were about as bad off."

"Have I been sleeping long?"

"You faded away back there when we were still running. That was late afternoon yesterday." Azlee nodded. The sun had already passed its zenith today.

She sighed, dreading the task that was now before her. Reaching into the pocket of her trousers, she pulled forth the talisman of evil. Pairey recoiled visibly.

"What are you doing?"

"We must destroy this, Pairey," Azlee replied in a quiet voice.

"We can wait until we reach another town. The chapel servants can help us then."

"No! It must be done now. We cannot bring this any farther, or we risk Al' Klathiu suffering the same fate as our southern neighbors."

"Fine. How can I help?"

Azlee leaned heavily against the sturdy oak which was currently serving as her spine. Pairey had nearly dragged her because she was too weak to help herself much at all. Now they both stood, staring at the malevolent stone in Azlee's palm.

"Do you think we could crush it?" Pairey asked, after a rather long silence.

"This thing survived the White Fire, Pairey. It can't be destroyed by ordinary means."

Pairey considered for a bit longer. "Do you have your Blessed Water with you?" Azlee nodded. "Hand it to me, please."

Pairey promptly upended the small bottle and dripped Blessed Water onto the talisman. A high-pitched shriek commenced which froze their blood and threatened to shatter their eardrums. A cloud of noxious smoke issued from the stone which was worse than the vilest privy mixed with old vomit and decaying critters. They clapped their hands to their ears desperately, but the bone-scraping screeching continued undiminished.

Just when Azlee felt sure she couldn't bear a second more, the sound ceased. The smoke dissipated, and the priestess and the brother were left staring at each other, white-faced and tight-lipped.

During an uneasy silence, Azlee's brain raced to find another possible solution to this quandary.

"Wait here with Akosha," she commanded. "I'll be gone a while. Don't follow me." Before Pairey could object, Azlee grabbed the pack with her robes stuffed inside and hurried off down the riverbank.

A blue-green pool shaded by regal oaks seemed perfect for Azlee's purpose. She stripped her body of her garments, ripe with sweat and long days in the saddle, and walked into the beckoning water. The cold liquid shocked her senses, forcing a temporary shiver.

The young priestess swam out to the middle of the pool where she floated on her back, letting the delicious cold take away her fatigue and worry for the moment. The points of her nipples became erect, surrounded by tiny goose bumps. Azlee smoothed her hands down her naked body, delighting in the silkiness of her skin, the soft thatch of light cinnamon hair below her abdomen. She closed her eyes. Now she must focus.

She sank deep into a trance. This time, instead of bending her will to achieve her own purpose, she offered her nubile young body for the pleasure of her powerful divine Husband. The union between the priestess and Edaru had only been consummated once in Azlee's life. A trembling little girl with huge brown eyes had managed to perform her part in her own marriage ceremony without error, after which the older girls had divested her of her white robes of high ritual. They had pushed her gently back onto the marriage bed, reserved for only these weddings, where her nakedness had confused and frightened her. They didn't leave her alone with her shame. They formed a circle around her, eyeing her like voyeurs, waiting for the god to claim his bride.

It seemed like an eternity that Azlee waited with pounding heart, not knowing what to expect and thoroughly humiliated. Suddenly, a sharp pain between her legs drew a startled cry from between her lips; her gaze flicked down and the crimson stain on the sheets elicited another cry. This was the point when she realized the other girls stood close enough to keep her from rising up out of the bed and fleeing. They kept pressing her thin shoulders against

56

the mattress so that she must lie still and endure this misery.

The very briefest moment of physical ecstasy followed that of the spilling of her virgin blood, and then it was over. Azlee's marriage to the god Edaru had been consummated.

Since that time when Azlee had lost her virginity to her divine husband at the tender age of nine, she had become an adult. She had acquired more knowledge about this sexual act between woman and god. Fear did not unsettle her this time as it had so long ago.

The warmth entered her between her legs. She spread them wide, lying on the surface of the still water which was her temporary marriage bed. A moan escaped her lips as ecstasy mounted within her. Her head was tilted back so that her chin faced the sky; her lips were parted and her breathing came in shallow pants.

After long moments of a physical rapture that Azlee had never imagined, her body returned to a state of peace and calm. She drifted over to the shore, climbed out of the pool, and dried herself with a musty cloth from her pack. She then slid her wrinkled white robe over her head. She felt wrong somehow, for allowing someone other than her beloved to possess her, even if it was the god she worshiped and trusted above all. She pushed these negative moods away with determination. Her sacrifice had been for the good of everyone, even the man she loved. She had done what she had no choice but to do.

Pairey's jaw dropped when he laid eyes on the

priestess walking purposefully toward him. He had lived among the wives of Edaru long enough to know that Azlee had lain with the god. Now His formidable spirit waited within Azlee's body until she called upon Him to lend her His power.

"What have you done?" he demanded, as soon as she was within earshot. "Only the High Priestess may lay with Edaru! It is sacrilege!"

"It is necessary!" Azlee returned hotly. "The High Priestess isn't here, and we must destroy the talisman! Do you know of a better way?"

Pairey remained silent.

"Good. Then let's get started." Using a pointed stick, the priestess drew upon the dry earth a diamond shape within a larger circle. In the center of the diamond, she placed the stone of evil, still carefully wrapped in her kerchief. Pairey cleansed his hands with a few drops of the Blessed Water, then placed a purple candle at each of the four points of the diamond as Azlee instructed. Incense smoldered between each candle to help drive out negative forces. As the smoke twisted upward, a new pungency was forged that included smoky cumin, sharp cloves, and soothing frankincense.

The priestess worked hard to still her racing heart and unsteady breathing. She must not be the young woman now. She was a priestess, wife of Edaru, and instrument of His will. She stood within the circle, but not inside the diamond shape with the thing of power. The circle would offer additional protection. The energy of the waiting god crackled within her. She held a pinch of bloodroot between her thumb and forefinger. One more moment and she tipped her head back and swallowed the waxy flower.

Potentially deadly, bloodroot also focused the inner energies. A few moments of deep breathing to boost her courage and calm her mind, and she could delay no further. She bent her will against the ugly talisman.

Digging a hole in the frozen earth with a spoon might have been easier. Grim, she pressed on. An object lacking free will, the talisman could not mount an offensive against its adversary. But Azlee's momentum must be maintained at all costs. Any pause, any hesitation, and she would lose any ground she gained against the dark stone. Azlee's strength would be depleted, making a second strike impossible.

When fatigue threatened to overwhelm her, she ruthlessly stripped every infinitesimal shred of energy from within her body. She clawed her way forward thrusting against the writhing wall of darkness.

Edaru's gift of power exhausted, Azlee's reserves drained, disorientation swept through her. Was she still within her own body? She no longer had any sensation of it. Spinning twisting her round and round, a malevolent maelstrom. She wanted to scream. *Make it stop!*

Horrified, she realized what was happening. She was being absorbed *into* the talisman. Frantic, she retreated. Too late, impossible to disengage.

I am Light! Her mind said, but the protest was feeble.

Her last tenuous hold on herself shuddered under the onslaught. She felt her powers ripped from her. She succumbed to the paralysis of fear.

* * *

Cold water was plunking down on her face, over and over. Thoroughly uncomfortable, she dragged her arm up to cover her closed eyes. Wait, hadn't she lost her physical form? Hadn't her soul merged with the evil of the talisman?

Apprehensive, she cracked open one eye. She found herself sprawled without grace across the ritual circle she had drawn what seemed like ages ago. The stone was gone from the center of the diamond. The incense no longer burned, though it still sweetened the air. The plopping drops of rain quickly soaked through her white robe. She propped herself up on her elbows, wondering when she was going to stop waking up disoriented and completely drained.

"What happened?" she managed when she saw Pairey coming toward her.

"You were losing the battle, Azlee," he began. She nodded. She had known as much.

He continued. "I had to try something. Anything. I held onto you with one hand and with the other I upended the bottle of Blessed Water onto it. While it was distracted, I dragged you out of the circle. I'm so sorry, Azlee, but I had to strike you several times to force you back into yourself. It was the only way."

Azlee touched her face. She felt the bruises tender along her cheekbone. "You don't have to apologize, Pairey. You saved my life." She reached up and clasped his hand in warm thanks for his bravery.

"We'd best move on now," Pairey said, suddenly brisk. "You two will catch your deaths out here in this rain."

Pairey had to lift Azlee into her saddle. Then he had to lift Akosha onto the saddle in front of him. The priestess had never before appreciated the humorless man as she did right now.

Chapter 8
Healing

The town of Rubek became the temporary residence of the priestess, the brother, and the outlander. A modest home just outside of the town became their shelter. Myrta, the wise woman of Rubek, who tended Edaru's chapel, had known of this house lying empty and insisted they make use of it while they recuperated. She refused to hear their protests, which were half-hearted anyway, since they knew they couldn't go much farther in their present bedraggled condition.

Myrta sent her pupil, a girl of plain features and quiet efficiency, to help the priestess and her companions. Before a full day passed, Azlee wondered how she'd ever gotten along without Enna.

Pairey looked at Azlee and jerked his head toward the front door. She glanced over at Enna. The girl's neck was bent, her rope of hair climbing down her back, while she focused her attention on preparing the evening's meal. No doubt it would be laced with strength-giving herbs as well as the meat and vegetables she'd bought at the small market. Enna didn't need the priestess now, so Azlee followed Pairey outside.

"We should go back to the Convent now," Pairey said.

"No. Akosha hasn't woken. I can't leave him like this."

"This girl can look after him. The wise woman can help, too. You've done your part to bring him to safety."

"I want to stay."

"There is no need. This is not your life, Priestess. You belong back at the Convent, in your proper role as the Consort of Edaru."

"You forget yourself, Pairey," Azlee said, deliberately hardening her voice. "Hear me now. I will not leave this man. I will stay for as long as is necessary. You, however, are quite free to leave at any time."

Before Pairey could formulate a response, Azlee turned smartly and removed herself from his presence.

She returned to her self-appointed post at Akosha's side. Ghostly, buried in a drift of blankets, his movement altogether arrested, Azlee's beloved had not regained consciousness even for a moment. In this state, he could not be made to eat. It was Enna who patiently cleaned him when he relieved himself in the bed.

Azlee cradled her hand inside Akosha's bigger one, still and cold. She crooned a wordless melody, a breathy, ethereal ballad within which her desperate heartache whispered and sighed. Her song was her plea and her prayer. Her song remained unanswered.

When she let her voice die, she realized Enna had moved to stand beside her. Without speaking, the younger girl folded the priestess into her arms. Azlee closed her eyes, appreciating the warmth and safety of this embrace.

"He is special to you," Enna said, when she had resumed her kitchen tasks. It was not a question.

Azlee nodded. It didn't even cross her mind to dissemble.

"To care for another is not an act of impiety, no matter which man or woman is the recipient of your regard. Does not your divine Master advocate for an open heart toward all, even those it is most difficult to love?"

Azlee nodded again. It was hard to find the words to reply to this rather unusual girl.

"Good. Then that's settled," Enna said, with brisk levity.

Azlee shook her head. *What* was settled? What on earth was Enna trying to say to her? But she ignored these questions that clamored inside her head, and opted for an observation instead.

"Your insight far exceeds your years," she remarked.

"I have been the wise woman's student from the time I was a small child. There were no other children to play with while I was growing up. I suppose much of who my teacher was rubbed off on me. Anyway, Myrta encouraged independent thinking even then."

"Did you choose to learn from Myrta?"

Enna cocked her head at the priestess. "I don't guess I did. Myrta wanted me for my potential. She asked for me. I was too young to say no."

"Did you ever want to return to your home and live with your parents again?"

"Perhaps at first. But I was kept busy with tasks and lessons. I loved learning, right from the start. I adapted easily to my new life. Priestess, it is easy to dream always of what might have been. What you must do is accept the life that is yours now, and take it as the gift it is."

It was the next day before Azlee had any more time to ponder Enna's words. She had risen just after dawn, too restless with doubt and anxiety to sleep. She crept outside to work out some of her tension with a walk.

It had rained again during the night. She slogged through the sodden grasses and shrubbery with no particular destination in mind. Despite herself, she was oddly energized by the fresh scent of newly laundered air and earth.

But the alluring summer landscape could not long distract the young priestess from her dilemma. Her head swirled with conflicting emotions, and sorting them out was proving to be a challenging undertaking. Destroying the evil talisman had nearly destroyed her. She would not have survived at all were it not for the gift of power from the Divine Sovereign and Pairey's urgency of thought and action. How then could she think of leaving her rank as priestess and Consort to Edaru? How could she repay her debt to the God of All by abandoning her responsibilities in pursuit of her own selfish pleasures? Though it broke her heart, she knew she must return to the Convent and resume her life as if she had never known Akosha. But she couldn't go without explaining it to him first.

Her despondent traipsing halted abruptly. She frowned for a moment, puzzled, before she actually smiled weakly, an action that felt rather unfamiliar by now.

"Priestess!" Enna's long legs drove her forward, rapidly closing the distance between them. "Priestess! He is awake!"

"What?" Enna grabbed Azlee's arm, pulling her back toward the house. Azlee gained her own momentum, bursting into the room where Akosha had long lay motionless. She barely noticed Pairey, leaning against a wall, watching their interaction.

Enna, not far behind her, plucked an empty teacup from Akosha's hand. No doubt she had ordered him to drink an infusion of healing herbs while she went for Azlee. The wise woman's pupil went out of the room to give them privacy. Pairey seemed to have no such consideration. Azlee ignored him.

"Hello," she rasped, around the unexpected lump in her throat. She settled down in her chair. "I've missed you."

The hand that reached to touch Azlee's pumpkin hair seemed nearly transparent. While she reveled in this touch she had feared she would never experience again, she grieved for the lost strength and virility in the man she loved.

Akosha dropped his hand, cradling hers within, as she had done for him these past days. "The evil in that place." He shuddered vehemently. She squeezed her hand in his. "Poisonous, insidious. My vulnerability exceeds that of most, and I couldn't help but succumb. It is my link to my land that makes it so. But the worst part was believing that I would never see you again." He paused. He seemed to be resting, gathering his strength. Even talking wore him out now. "Azlee, my love. You saved me. You brought me back to the Light."

"Of course," she replied. Why did she want to sob now, when her dear one was finally safe? "I couldn't leave you there. It broke my heart just knowing the pain you were in."

"My pack. Please, I need my pack."

Akosha reached into the pack Azlee handed him. When he set the pack aside, his fist hid an object. He opened his palm. Azlee's breathing paused. She couldn't remove her eyes from the exquisite ring displayed on Akosha's hand. All of nature's colors intermingled in a serene celebration of life and love and Light. Azlee recognized that the stone comprising this ring was identical to that which formed the amulet Akosha had shown her on one of their first evenings together.

"Do you like it?" he asked. "I had it made for you before I went back. I thought it would bring me luck. It seems it did."

Azlee should have noticed the nervous tone to his conversation. He had always been so relaxed with her. But the power of the stone bewitched her.

"It is gorgeous, of course, Akosha," she breathed.

He let go of Azlee's right hand, reaching with both of his hands to take her left one. "Priestess Azlee of Al'Klathiu, will you marry me?"

An explosion behind her distracted her from answering right away.

"You fool!" Pairey spluttered. "Priestesses are forbidden to marry."

Akosha's crumpled face echoed his crushed dream. Azlee shot to her feet, whirling to face Pairey.

"Get out!" she yelled. Pairey didn't even argue, though the look he threw her way seethed with rebellion.

Alone with her dear one at last, Azlee stretched out beside him on the bed, her head against his shoulder.

"I'm sorry," he whispered. His voice was ragged. "I thought it was what you wanted."

She propped herself up on one elbow so she could look into his eyes. "Akosha, my love, it *is* what I want."

He grinned, but it was a cautious grin. "Then priestesses are not forbidden to marry?"

"No, that part is true. Priestesses are forbidden to marry."

He stared at her.

"Love, Edaru released me from my commitment to Him. It happened just before Enna came to tell me you were awake. Then He kissed my forehead and let me go." She paused for a moment to relive that beautiful moment. "He wants me to be free to choose you, and I do. I will always love Him, but I can have you both in my life."

The doubt finally vanished from Akosha's face. He whooped. He gathered Azlee into his arms. "I love you, Azlee. So much."

Chapter 9
Choices

Grim and gray as it had always been, the Convent seemed more appalling than previously, to Azlee's jaded eye. Nevertheless, she slid off Mare's back, brushed the dirt off her pale green riding skirts, and entered the ugly stone building.

She strode purposefully but without haste up the main hall. The Priest-Mother sat in her usual chair, the place where she received visitors. Kishrion stood behind her, immaculate and icy as always. Neither said anything as they eyed their defector priestess. Their faces were twin masks.

Azlee reached the two women and slung a pack on the floor near them. "These are my robes, my cloaks, my symbols of office. I no longer need them."

"You whore!" Kishrion burst out. "How dare you step into this place after what you've done!"

"Hush, Kishrion," Priest-Mother ordered, gesturing for silence.

Kishrion obeyed, glaring at Azlee.

"Child," Priest-Mother said, fastening her gaze on Azlee. "Go in peace. May Edaru light your way. Always."

Azlee clenched her teeth to keep her jaw from diving for the floor. Priest-Mother was not going to fight her on this? She nodded, according the older woman a short bow in respect and gratitude. "Thank you, Priest-Mother."

In Rubek, Pairey had been so angry his eyes seemed ready to pop out of his head. His face had turned the most startling shade of crimson.

"You stupid, thoughtless girl!" he'd ranted at her. "I knew you thought I was blind, you thought I couldn't see how you looked at him! But I never thought you would take it this far! You are the Consort of the God of All! You will shame him, breaking your vow to satisfy the heat in your loins!"

By now, Azlee had heard far more than enough. She had some screaming of her own to do. "Don't you talk to me like that, grumpy old man! All you care about is panting like a dog to the Priest-Mother, hoping she'll pat you on the head and say good boy! You know nothing about love, about passion, about following your heart. You're a coward! A coward! You're afraid to really live, that's the real reason you're raging at me."

There had been more heated words exchanged, but Azlee grew tired of the fight. She had sent

Pairey away with a promise that she herself would go before the Priest-Mother. *She* would not play the coward.

He waited for her beside Mare. "Hello, Azlee." His voice was calm. Like they had not exchanged heated, hurtful words nearly two weeks ago.

"Hello, Pairey," she replied. "What are you doing here?"

"I live here. And I wanted to see you."

"Why?"

"There's something I want to tell you."

"Oh, Pairey, do you still want to argue about this? Let me tell you something. This is not your fault. I made my own decision, and you couldn't change my mind. You've got to let this go."

"That's not what I want to talk about."

"It's not?"

"I'm sorry I got angry. I'm sorry for all the hurtful things I said to you. The truth is, you're a bright, beautiful woman, with tremendous courage. I've known you since the first day you came here. I could see how smart you were even then. And how unhappy. But later, you seemed to find yourself. You seemed content. See, I was mad at you because I didn't want to see you lonely and sad like you were back then. I wanted you to be happy, and was worried about you making the wrong choice. I should have trusted you. I'm sorry."

"You're forgiven, Pairey. And I want you to know I admire you. For your bravery, your quick thought, your strength. I thought you were boring before all this started, but I learned respect for you in our terrifying little adventure together." She laughed. Pairey laughed too.

"Have a happy life, Azlee," he said. He hugged her.

Riding on toward her rendezvous with Akosha, she couldn't keep the smile from curving her lips. Kishrion had wanted to scandalize her, to humiliate her as had been her habit for long years, but Priest-Mother of all people had stopped her. Kishrion had to be writhing in her agony, for she would never get another opportunity. And Azlee was going on to a life of happiness.

Leaving Enna had proved to be difficult. Much affection had grown in Azlee for the intelligent, young woman who had given Azlee the female support she so desperately needed. Both women shed tears upon parting, alleviated somewhat only by exchanged promises to visit each other often.

Akosha nearly pulled her off Mare's back when she rode into the courtyard of the inn where he waited without patience for her. He threw his arms around her, landing a kiss on her lips. She burst out laughing.

"What is it?" he demanded. "Are you laughing at me?"

Azlee shook her head, still bubbling over. "It's just—I'm so happy to be here with you."

He grinned back. "That makes two of us." He slid his arm around her slender waist, drawing her forward with him. "Didn't you say you had news for me?"

She nodded. "It was the Sight that showed me. Sarronel and his men destroyed the Shadowed militia. They won!"

"We won," he corrected.

"We did, didn't we?" He grew blurry to her through her delighted tears.

"Yes we did. Come on, then. It's time to get married."

CPSIA information can be obtained at www.ICGtesting.com
Printed in the USA
BVOW01s1416200114

342463BV00001B/28/P

9 781432 730109